His thoughts...
Her thighs

"His thoughts are always between her thighs..."

BetrayalBooks.com Presents

His thoughts...

Her thighs

v.2

BetrayalBooks.com

Copyright ©2012 by Myra P. Lovett

All rights reserved.

Please visit my website at www.BetrayalBooks.com

Printed in the United States of America

First printing: November 2012

ISBN-13: 978-0-9828628-1-0

ISBN-10: 0982862814

Dedicated to JuNiPh...with love!

Always...and again!!!!

Warning:

This book is for entertainment purposes and retirement purposes only. This book is not for the faint of heart. If you have any of the following conditions, please put this book down and run for your life!

Conditions:

Weak heart

Jealousy issues

Holier than thou

Married and have a hard time accepting that married men sleep around

Have a problem with misspelling, mispunctuations or other proof reading issues...

THIS BOOK AIN'T FOR YOU!

But if it is for you, enjoy it and pass it along!!! I'm ready to retire! ☺

Prologue

From:

"The bitch that you hate to LOVE!"

Welcome back bitches! First of all, I want to thank all of you who have read the first book and thoroughly enjoyed it. Thank you for actually taking time out of your life to read my story! So right now I'm sitting here trying to figure out what the hell I want to say in this prologue but I just realized that this is the conclusion to volume 1. And you're wondering what the fuck does that mean? That means that I don't have to give a long, drawn out, tear jerking opening to this book.

On that note, let's get to the point. What you bitches really want to know is what happened to my "half-brother" Thomas, what happened at the wedding and the big question is who the fuck does this big headed ass baby belongs to. Well...here it is okay. And don't expect greatness to this shit.

It's just a straight to the point story and... here's volume 2 and I hope that you will enjoy it like the first one. And if not, well...you're not getting your money back!

Doing what I do best...sucking and fucking...

Yours truly,

Delilah

P.S. There is not a lot of sex in this volume...for you perverted ass readers!!!!

Another Funeral:
The Nephew finally thinks
(Tim)

2

(Tears welling in my eyes…)

Unc is dead. Dead as hell but at least he went out with a bang…literally. I just can't believe that a week ago we were on the boat chilling at the lake and now we're burying him. (Shaking my head) It seems so unreal and I feel like my heart is going to break but I'm going to make it through this…with the help of my family and Delilah.

(Gripping Delilah's hand…)

She's been a blessing ever since I met her and I'm going to ask her to be my wife….tonight. I know all of this is so soon but with Unc dying and things going the way they are going, I need to settle down and get right with God and her. But that's another story at another time. Right now I'm focusing on Auntie C is sitting in front of me and she's crying like…. an ugly ass baby that just fell down the steps. Yeah…Auntie C is pretty ugly crying like that. She shouldn't look like that…ever.

Damn… (wiping a tear from my eye)…it breaks my heart to see her so upset but it's nothing that I can do for her…not now. I want to talk to her about that night but I'll have to wait. She really hasn't spoken to me about Unc's death and I don't want to upset her any more than what she already is…but we must talk.

I don't want Auntie C to think or believe that I knew about his secret sex life because I didn't. I mean I knew about all of the other women that he was seeing on the side but I'm just as surprised to find out that Unc liked it up the dookey shoot. Man…I'm getting sick just thinking about that.

(Slightly gagging….)

4

Reminiscing Alert*Reminiscing Alert***

Well the day after family day on the lake, Unc told me that he had some errands to run so no one really knew where he was going. Although he likes to have fun and be around a lot of people, there are times when he just really needed his privacy. And this particular day was one where he didn't tell anyone where he was going...until I got his text.

Around 7 pm I got a message from him that said **"I need help. Come to room 223 at Baby Nuts Inn but don't tell anyone! The key is under the mat!"** My stomach fell because I knew that something was terribly wrong. Unc never texts me. So I jumped up from my bed and put on my clothes because at the time he sent me the message, I was laying in my room naked ...stroking my dick...getting ready to masturbate. So I got dressed and left without telling anyone where I was going and no one asked either.

About 30 minutes later, I arrived at Baby Nuts Inn but I had to ask the lady at the desk how to get to room 223 in which she replied "Up the hill…and around the back." in her Alvin the chipmunk voice. I thanked her, rushed out the door, got back in my car, drove up the hill and around the back to get to his room. Luckily there were no cops or anyone else there but I secretly wished there were. My stomach was in a knot and I began to get really nervous. My heart was racing as I took the key from the mat but I knew that I had to work quick…I had to help my dear uncle so I opened the door and I wasn't prepared for what I saw! **(That was a WTF moment…like I've never experienced before!)**

I ran to the bed and I shook him…"Unc, Unc…wake up!" but he didn't respond. I felt his pulse which was none. I tried to turn him over to give him CPR but there was a problem…he had a fake dick up his ass which wouldn't let me put him flat on his back. So I had to do the unthinkable…I went to take the fake dick out of his ass but he shitted on it. But I didn't care cause that's my uncle…he's like my father so as I was removing the dildo out of his ass…the cops busted through the door with their guns out yelling **"Put the dick down and your hands up!"**…

"This is not what you think!" I yelled at the cops...but I dropped the fake dick and stood up with my hands raised. "Can I at least wash the shit off of my hands?" I asked as I trembled in fear. And they let me...wash my hands and explain to them what was going on. While I was talking to them, the ambulance had arrived but they pronounced him dead on arrival. I cried hysterically like a bitch who just got slapped and I fell to the floor because I couldn't believe that my uncle was dead....what I really couldn't believe was that Unc was gay but the proof...

While the cops were looking around the room, I saw the porn magazine on the bed with him and I was hoping that this was a sick joke, but it wasn't. Damn! So after all of that, they finally called Auntie C to the hotel to verify who I was and to identify my uncle. I think that was the toughest moment right there because I didn't want her to know about his secret. I didn't think that she could've handled it but when she arrived she took it like a champ. She verified who I was and she identified his body....then she just walked out. I thought that was unusual but she just left and said absolutely nothing. Not a fucking teardrop nor a hello....

**Reminiscing is over...Back at the funeral! **

So here we are...at Unc's funeral and I just feel so guilty. I haven't told anyone about what I saw in the hotel except for Delilah. I didn't want to tell her but I couldn't hold it in. I just feel like I could have done more. I should've called 911 when I left the house, but (sigh)....

And Auntie C...she never asked me why I was there. I don't know if she's upset with me, but I don't know what to tell her...I'm at a loss for words.

But now that I think about it...who the hell called the cops?

Dear God,

Please forgive me. Please! I know that I was wrong but I don't believe that I was that wrong. (Sigh)....Damn. I feel so bad for Uncle Bobby. Look at him up there in his casket. Poor baby...but he looks at peace. And his poor wife...bless her God and hold her near! I know she's going through it.

I know that she thinks he was gay and I wish I could tell her that he wasn't but I can't tell on myself. Sometimes I scare myself...how I'm able to get out of these lies and I can't believe how dumb his nephew is but I'm thankful that he is. If he was smarter then he would've figured out that it was **"I WHO CALLED THE COPS!"** Anyway this is what really happened to his old ass wrinkled dick uncle.....

(Reminiscing time...your ass should know by now)...

I got a call around 3 in the afternoon to meet Uncle Bobby at Baby Nuts Inn in room 223 as you know. So when I got there we talked, laughed and got high for a while. Then we started to fuck and fuck and fuck but then we did our usual in which I carefully rammed a fake dick up his old ass. Now I don't know why the old man was freaky as hell...he never said he was gay or anything so hey... I strongly believe in don't ask don't tell.

Anyway, I felt a little bad (just a little) because all of this is kind of my fault. He told me to replace the batteries and well...I forgot to change them from our last love session. Well unfortunately for him the batteries went dead which did something to the dildo in his ass and right at that very same moment, Uncle Bobby screamed, ejaculated and fell out....all at the same time.

(Sighing)….

Unfortunately for me, he died at the very moment the damn batteries went out….they died together. Those fucking batteries…I thought they kept going. Anyway, come to find out later on through his autopsy that there was some type of electrical shortage in the dildo that caused the battery in his pacemaker to stop and well that's what killed him. I don't suppose to know that but his nephew told me since he's the one who found Unc.

"I know I shouldn't be laughing, but I can't help it!"

Yours truly…I. Lovett

(Back to the story…)

So there he was on the bed…dead…with a fake dick shoved up his ass…and a smile on his face. I didn't have to worry about his eyes being open because they were shut…from his orgasm. But what I did have to worry about was him shitting on himself because you know…once they die they shit. That meant that I only had a few minutes to work with him so I threw on my clothes and luckily I had a pair of fucking latex gloves in my purse (don't ask).

I put the gloves on and got a few towels from the bathroom and wiped everything …well the stuff that I touched. I wasn't concerned about the dildo…I figured by the time the shit got on it, well there wouldn't be any finger prints to find. Anyway, I did a good job by not panicking. I almost did but I didn't. What I decided to do next…well that's where I got a little nervous.

Instead of calling the cops at that moment, I went to the store and purchased a gay male magazine. I figured this would throw them off of my trail since old man winter already had a dick shoved up his anus. So I went back to the hotel and laid the magazine open on the bed…in front of him. I also put his hand around his dick…to make it look like he was masturbating.

I removed his condom, wrapped it in the towel that I used and took it with me because I didn't want to take a chance with my DNA being detected. I then took his phone (yes he's shitted by now but I handled the stench) and sent his nephew the text from his cell phone. The text said **"I need help. Come to room 223 at Baby Nuts Inn but don't tell anyone! The key is under the mat."** And I got the fuck on.

And I didn't worry about my phone being traced because I have one of those Dollar Family phones so when I'm in situations like these, I can just throw the phone away. But before I threw the phone away I went ahead and called the cops. I didn't want his nephew to get in trouble but I knew that they had to get Unc's old ass up out of there. I thought that I had given my boyfriend enough time to get the magazine and dick out of his ass before the cops got there but apparently I didn't.

(Reminiscing over...Back at the funeral)....

So now I need a cigarette. I'm crying and shit but it's not for real. I just have to play the fucking grieving girlfriend. But if this motherfucker next to me ever found out, well ...he won't. Even if he did, he wouldn't believe it so I'm not worried. "I'm going to smoke a cigarette. I'll be back." ...I told him as I walked out of the church. And while I was walking I saw Uncle Bobby's grandson...yeah the 3 year old...with a small band aid on his lip...ugh! I hope it's just a scratch!

Uncle Tommy...at the
funeral...

14

Man...damn. My road dog...my ace...my brother-in-law....dead. This just can't be...it just can't be real but it is! **(Tears welling up...)** I'm not going to cry right now but I have cried....with Delilah. I know this hasn't been the right time but I needed some sex. I called her last night after the wake and she met me at the Baby Nuts Inn...room 223. The room was nice and the clerk told me that the room had a brand new mattress. She explained that they were doing some upgrades and that room was picked as one of the one's to get a mattress upgrade. She also said that "No one has slept on that mattress...we just replaced it yesterday!"

So it made me feel good to know that Delilah and I were the first...to fuck on the mattress. So we did our thing last night and I feel so much better. I'm still hurt but my stress level is down. But she's sitting directly behind me which means that I can't see her but it's all good. I have the memory of last night freshly baked in my mind.

Anyway, I'm taking a chance right now pretending to look at the back door and I see Delilah walking out. I just hope everything is okay but I can't call her right now. I just hope that she's not taking Unc's death too hard. I wonder where she's going but I am worried about her. Last night she confided in me that she was worried about my nephew. My phone just buzzed…I hope that it's her…

(Checking my phone…just got a text)…

I know this isn't the right time for this but that was Delilah who just text me….and I love my brother-in-law…may he RIP, but I have a question…

Would it be wrong for me to meet Delilah…in the church bathroom…to get my dick sucked?

Damn. I hate a man that can't make up his mind on his own. Apparently he didn't think it was wrong because he got his old ass up and came to the bathroom...and he came...in my mouth. But anyway, I think I'm addicted to giving head.

Maybe I'm wrong but I've come to the realization that I suck a lot of dick. But I just really enjoy pleasuring a man orally. It turns me on but I don't have to explain that shit. I am who I am and that's all that matters. And as for last night, having sex with Unc's brother-in-law in the same room where he died...that was not my choice. Purely coincidental...I almost passed out when I had to go back to that room.

Thank God they replaced that old ass mattress.

Delilah.

Thomas:
Half- brother Blues

(Watching the ceiling)...

Right now I'm back in her bed. I finally came out the bathroom and we had our much needed talk afterwards. I told her how bad I was feeling about sleeping with her since we are related. We both decided that we should finish what we've started and that I should just fuck her for the rest of the night. So I just sent a text to my wife letting her know that I was too drunk to drive home.

She just text me back and said, "Why don't you just stay at your sister's house tonight. The kids and I are fine. ☺" That's why I love her... she's so fucking naïve. Anyway...let me get my freak on with my half-sister for one last time. She just sat on the back of my head...shining my scalp...with her pussy. Such a great feeling...

(45 minutes later)....

Right now Delilah is holding me....and my nuts....in her mouth. (Just kidding...she's massaging my balls with her hands). But I'm still going through fits about finding out about my dad. She finally explained to me that our dad isn't my father and that he chose to keep that a secret so I wouldn't get hurt.

As much as I want to be pissed off about this whole situation…I'm not. I'm actually relieved because I wouldn't have had the best sex in my life if it wasn't for them. So mom and dad…I salute you! Thank you for the lie but more importantly…thank you Big Mama for sharing the lie with Delilah before your ass went senile. Anyway, she's giving me a hand/blow job now…I'll be back.

(10 minutes later…)

I just came in her mouth and right now she's in the bathroom brushing her teeth. I feel like a brand new man, but I've got to get me some damn rest. All this sucking and fucking we've been doing has made me tired as hell. But it's been wonderful I must admit.

So after the big revelation, Delilah and I both decided that we would continue to see each other sexually on the side but I asked her not to tell my wife that she's not my half-sister. We both agreed that its best that my wife stays clueless know so it would be easy for us to be with each other…without any suspicion. I mean hell…who would ever suspect that I'm fucking my **"half-sister"**?

(Delilah's back in bed…)

I just rolled her fine ass over on her back and now I'm eating her meow mix (her pussy for those of you who don't get it). And she's going wild. Her legs are up in the air and trembling like a child scared of their daddy. So I'm gonna keep doing what I'm doing. I'm gonna keep eating her until her pussy blows in my mouth like a hand grenade.

Also, it's a real treat to be able to see her suck on her own nipples (yes her tits are that big…damn) while I eat her out. I wish my wife could do that…but she can't…her breasts are all dried up like raisins due to the kids. Fucked up visual huh? Yeah I know but that's my fucking life…with my wife. But let me get back focused and keep eating her fat juicy pussy…with her fine ass.

(Tongue wrestling her pussy...and I'm winning)...

"Oh my! Excuse me"...she just said as she stopped sucking on her tits. She's looking kind of bewildered but I'm still eating her out. I can't take my mouth off of her pussy...not now. But it just hit me...I realize why she looks like that...she just farted...while my face is between her legs.

Fuck it…its Delilah and her fart smells like ground up peaches. "No problem baby! Relax!" and I'm back to eating her out. Her pussy is so fucking juicy…… I think she's about to cum…she's grabbing my head and now she's yelling my name…

"Thomas, Thomas!"…..and now her legs are shaking harder and the inside of her thighs are sweaty. This shit is such a turn on. I wish that y'all could see her right now…better yet I wish that yall could put your mouth on her fat pussy. But since you can't, I'm just going to keep licking her fat cat like a bowl of 2 percent milk…but I want to hear my name again. And there she blows……she's coming and she screams my name again…

"Thomas, Thomas!…."
Yesssssssssssssssssssssssssss….

23

Wake up dear! Your sister is at the front door."…my wife said…always fucking with my thoughts…now she's interrupting my fucking dreams!

(Up from my nap…opening the front door)…

My half- sister just walked in and now she's back in my arms (she's hugging me). It's been about a month since we've seen each other and I have sorely missed her. "You need to let me go before your wife gets suspicious" she just whispered in my ear. "Oh yeah…you're right" as I whispered back to her because I totally forgot about my wife.

Anyway, I just let her go and she's walking into the living room. I couldn't help it but I had to turn around and watch her. (She's fine as hell!) My wife just walked in the living room with her and they are talking but this time I decided that I would just sit here and listen to them instead of going off to masturbate.

She just told me that she has a surprise for my half-sister. My beautiful but yet pitiful ass wife…. I wonder what the hell she has in store. "Well Delilah….I know you said that you're not looking for anyone but I know this wonderful man who would be perfect for you." …she's telling Delilah.

"What the fuck are you doing?" I wanted to yell at her but instead I'm asking "Who are you introducing her to dear?" I want to chop her in the throat out right now but I have to be calm but I'm actually getting jealous. And the words that she just said made me almost choke this bitch…

"Well dear, I know that you want only the best for your little sister so I decided to introduce her to Tiso…your **half-brother**." And at this very moment I wish that I could choke this bitch.

(Doorbell rings)…

She's saved by the motherfucking bell.

Tiso
The First Visit

(At my brother's front door...)

Shit...I'm nervous as hell. I don't really like
blind dates but his wife said that I would be
pleasantly surprised about this one. The
situation is kind of unusual because the woman
that I'm meeting is actually my half-brother's
half-sister. But she and I aren't related.

My brother and I have the same mother but we
have different fathers. But they have the same
father but different mothers. And I've never met
Delilah. So technically we're not related...I
don't think we are. This shit sounds kind of
tricky but oh well...I'm here now.

(Door opens)...

"What's up Tiso...bring your ass on in." my
brother says but he seems to be upset. "What's
up with you Thomas? Are you upset about
something? "I replied as I'm walking into his
house. "Hi T...nice flowers!" his wife says as
she comes up to me with her arms open. I'm
hugging her now but she's holding me pretty
tight...what's up with that.

Anyway, she's letting me go and we're walking into the living room where she says that she's going to "introduce me to one of the finest women I've ever seen". "I thought you had a girlfriend Tiso?" my half –brother yelled out.

"I haven't had one of those in a long time…you know this."…I replied. What the fuck is his problem? Anyway, I'm finally in the living room and his wife introduces me to her… this chocolate candy bar of a woman who is standing at the fireplace looking at me looking at her. I see the face of an angel, the body of a Goddess and a hard on that was about to bust out of my fucking pants. And it hits me…

"I'm Delilah! Nice flowers" …she says to me and then she flashes me a come and lick my pussy smile. But for some odd reason I feel the need to play stupid and act like this is the first time we've met…because this isn't. I just can't remember where I know her from.

"Hi…I'm Tiso. These flowers are for you! "…I said as I just handed her the flowers. She's thanking me right now with a nice hug and a wet kiss on the cheek. And at that very moment when her soft lips met my cheek, I remembered exactly who she is and where we met…and what we did! How could I forget a dick sucker like that but something is throwing me off. First of all, I had no fucking idea that she's my half-brother's half-sister. And the second thing is….**her name is Salisa.**

(Listening to Beethoven…with a glass of Chardonnay…reading "99 ways to masturbate…1 way to cum" by I. Lovett)….

Yes….he knows who I am…and I definitely know who the fuck he is. We just didn't know that we had the same half-brother. And yes he's right about my name. I don't tell everyone my real name is Delilah. I met him at a bar and we had a one night, well an all-day …**fuckarama**!!!! I met him a couple of years ago… and let's just say…both of the brothers have very big dicks!!!! But Tiso is a lot finer than Thomas.

I could tell you more about his half-brother, but it's such a long drawn out story that I really don't want to talk about it right now. But thankfully he knew not to say anything when he saw me. I didn't want my and I quote "our half-brother" to know what our previous relationship was like.

And as for my half-brother, well he certainly dreams a lot. But for the record, yes we've fucked and we are currently fucking. Also, I want to let y'all know that his wife is not ugly and her tits aren't dried up like grapes.

I don't have time to tell y'all how the fuck I know this, but trust me I know. She has some very nice breasts and her nipples are large...and golden brown. Hmmmm...I've said too much. That's another story...another day...another book.

Delilah.

Poor
Nigel...
(A month later)...

(Driving)...

I'm on my way from work and I must admit that I miss her...Delilah that is. I haven't seen or spoken to her since I left...the day that my wife had our son. I just couldn't lie to her because it was killing me. So to keep me from lying to her, I haven't spoken to Delilah in a month. I love her but I'm scared to call, but I will text her soon. I hope that she won't be too upset about all of this but I'm going to tell her the truth and hopefully she will accept me and my situation. Besides that, I'm hornier than two goats. I need some of that good head she gives...so I'll just text her when I get home.

Anyway my wife just text me...."Dinner and a movie are waiting!" Yeah...hip hip fucking hooray...another fucking movie night with me her and the kid. What a life...but I'm stuck with her...in this lifeless marriage. I'm from Africa and I only married her to stay in this country. I actually paid her to marry me but when I went to get the divorce, she threatened to tell immigration about our arrangement so that's why we're together.

It's all fucked up but I will deal with it because I don't want to go back. I don't love her and we barely have sex but I just try to make her happy the best way I can. "Be home soon ☺"…is my reply but I'm taking the long route home.

(Finally home…walking through the door)…

"I'm home dear…" I said but I didn't get a reply. I'm putting my stuff down on the table and realize that she didn't say anything. "I'm home dear. What did you cook for dinner?" Let me walk in the kitchen and see what she cooked.

(In the kitchen...at the stove)...

Now why would she fucking text me and say "dinner and a movie" with no fucking dinner made? What the fuck is going on...

(Walking up these long ass stairs and hungry as hell)...

"Where's dinner?"...I'm trying not to yell but I'm sick of these games that she plays. "Where are you?" I asked her and I'm walking in our room. Surprise, surprise...I'm about to fucking fall out!

"Welcome home sweet dick!"...... is what I heard, but what I saw was fucking unbelievable!

Wow! I wonder what the fuck did he see. I'm very curious. I mean what could be so fucking unbelievable for his lame ass to see? Could it be that I was laying in his bed masturbating while his baby laid next to me sleep? Naw…I wouldn't do that. (smiling)… Could it possibly be that I was breastfeeding the little kid while mommy was at work? Naw…you know I wouldn't do that shit. ;-) Maybe it was this shit that he saw…you've been warned bitches.

****Reminiscing Alert***Reminiscing Alert***

I wish you could've seen the look on his face when he saw me lying on his bed…butt naked as hell…with his baby laying next to me sleep. And his wife, well let's just say she was speechless…meaning that her head was between my legs…eating pussy pie. That shit was priceless.

He looked like he had seen a ghost after he realized what the fuck was going on. Then he left the house and I don't know where the fuck he went. She went after him but she realized that I wasn't going to keep the brat. So I got dressed and pretended to go after his ass for her….but I knew where he was going.

I took my ass home and that's where I found him outside of my home…crying like the bitch that he is. I walked up to the passenger side of his car door, knocked on the window and he let me. He was crying and said he was hurt and needed to know how his wife and I hooked up. I politely explained to him that his wife and I became buddies…the night that she took my nude photos, we just hit it off and that's when we started seeing each other as friends.

He couldn't stop crying and begged to understand why I would do this to him. "Why Delilah? You cause me much grief and pain! You know I love you…don't you?"…he spoke in his Nigerian African dark and lovely accent. "Well…no I don't know that you love me. I haven't seen your ass in a month."…I replied.

I went on to tell him that I let his wife eat my pussy to get back at him for not calling me and then I pretended to cry. **(Motherfuckers fall for that shit every damn time.)** Feeling guilty for all the pain he caused, he started to hug me and apologized. Then he kissed me and promised that he would never hurt me again....damn sucker.

So we went up to my place and we fucked the night away. I got to get some of that good old African dick and his wife...well she got to taste my good ol' American apple pussy pie...freshly shaven. And yes...I made him eat the pussy pie as well...his wife eats pussy better. ☺

After we got through fucking, he apologized again for not calling me in a whole fucking month but he said he was confused. He also explained that he and his wife were in a messed up arranged marriage so I forgave him and in return he forgave me for letting his wife eat my cooch....cause I didn't put my mouth on her shit. I don't roll like that.

Dick sucker for life!

Delilah!

Back from mini-vacation:
Sam~step dad...sick
thoughts!

We just got back in town from Savannah and we're back at the house. The nurse has finally left and my wife is sleeping well in our bed. Right now I'm taking my clothes off… Delilah and I are fucking one more time before I tend to my wife. So I'm getting my dick sucked as you are reading this and in about 10 minutes after she swallows about a pound of nut that's coming out of me…I'm going to fuck my step daughter 5 ways from Sunday so y'all just hold tight while I get it in…

(2 hours later…)

Well we just finished fucking and I have something that I must admit to you. I hate to say this but Delilah and I have a fetish…a very sick fetish. See the reason why my wife was sleep is…well the problem is that my wife, which is Delilah's mom as you know, well she was in a freakish accident about 6 months ago.

Sooooooooo....the accident kind of fucked her up meaning that it left her paralyzed, deaf, and blind which means she can't move any of her limbs, she can't see and she can't hear.
Yeah that's pretty fucked up but I'm doing my best to stay by her side...literally.

One day, about a couple of months after the accident, when her mother came home, Delilah and I assessed the situation and that's when we both realized that we could do whatever we wanted in my wife's bed and she wouldn't know shit.   After that revelation, whenever Delilah comes over, we've been...well we've been fucking in her mom's room (yes with her mom in the bed).

At first, it started with Delilah sucking my dick while I was sitting on the side of the bed with her mother. I would hold my wife's hand while I shot off in Delilah's mouth, but then it just got to be so exciting and then it got kinkier and I just couldn't get enough of fucking in the room...in the same bed with my wife...without her knowing.

So now we fuck in here all the time. I mean we get to scream, yell, and walk around naked while my wife knows nothing. Plus the doctor said that I should be near my wife most of the time so this benefits my wife as well as me. We get to keep our eyes on her so it's a win-win situation for all three of us.

And boy have we been fucking. **(Smiling)** Delilah's favorite position is doggy style. Yes she likes it when she's at the end of the bed while she holds her mother's ankles while I fuck her from the back. Yeah I know I'm going to hell...and I pray to God every day to help me. Will you pray for me too? Please. I need fucking help but it's something about Delilah that just makes me do anything....well just about anything.

He can't keep his fucking mouth shut if someone paid him. Okay…**(puffing on a cigarette)** I know that it's bad enough that I'm fucking my step-dad. I get that…okay. But fucking my step-dad while my mother lies in bed because she can't hear…she can't see…she can't move. That makes me seem just cruel, but I need for you to hear me out. Don't judge me just yet…

The deal with my mom is we got into a heated argument that day. I mean I love my mom and all but our relationship has been…well not a good one. Anyway, she stormed out of the house and I tried to stop her, but she didn't listen to me. I told her "Ma….you can't drive a stick shift with a cane." But she didn't listen…and she got into a horrible accident which left her in this condition.

Hold on for a second…I need some tissue to wipe my tears and blow my nose. This is just so sensitive to me.

(Wiping tears…blowing my nose)…

Okay I'm back. I had a break down but I'm okay…I'm really okay.

Anyway, I know that my step dad is trying to put all the blame on me, but he's the one who suggested that we have sex next to Ma. But the bed is a California King so it's not like we were bothering her. But the idea of me holding her ankles while we were fucking was my idea. His sick ass always said that he wanted to be in a threesome. Ugh…I need prayer player…will y'all pray for me too?

Please?

Delilah.

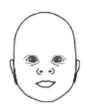

Dave's Big headed Ass
Baby...
Who's your mammy?!

45

(Next day...back at the hospital)....

Coochie coo...awe...look at his big headed ass. He's so handsome but I'm having doubts about if he's mine or not. I mean my God his head is so fucking big. Anyway, I don't want to start thinking like that. My baby's mama has been very supportive of me and my situation. She hasn't done anything to try to break up my home so I don't want to start shit with her. I really don't want to give her any reason to contact my wife about this child. **(Still holding his big headed ass)** Shhh...he's gone back to sleep now so I'm taking him back to the nursery. And then I will visit her before I leave. I'll be right back.

(An hour later...)

Somehow she managed to give me some of that good ass head right before she went into the hospital room so I appreciate that. But we finally got a chance to talk about everything. She told me that's she's very disappointed in the fact that I haven't told my wife about her.

"Babe…I have a lot of shit going on right now."
I told her. I mean what the fuck does she want
from me? It's fucking stressful to even think
about how I'm going to tell my wife about my
outside child. She knows this and right now
she's yelling and putting this damn demands on
me, but not only does she want me to tell my
wife about her….she wants me to go into the
room and tell her fucking sister that we're
fucking. Yeah…her sister is my baby mama and
she is…well y'all know who the fuck she is.
She's Delilah…the "head" nurse.

Sorry folks…I'm not the fucking mammy. Don't need a DNA test for this one. I know that I am capable of many things, but having this man's child…never. It just so happens that my baby sister would be the one to actually have a kid with a married man. And look at the results…my nephew's head is big and well…let's just say that he's the rotten apple of her eye…he's not cute. He may grow out of that shit, but right now…he's UGhh…ly!

But let me get to the point. I've only been fucking him for…8 months now. I met him when my sister introduced us…right after she found out that she was pregnant. And yes I care about him…but I care about my baby sister more and I think that she should know that we are fucking.

I just don't want to be the one to tell her. I'm not telling her shit...she's crazy about him. She's going to be hurt but she doesn't have the right to be. She has fucked around with a couple of my ex-boyfriends soooooooo....we all know payback is a bitch.

I figured that if he's going to tell his wife about his baby with my sister, then he might as well tell his wife about me as well. And then while he's taking himself through hell, well he might as well let the cat out of the fucking bag to my sister. So, because that motherfucker can lick both of my ass cheeks, that is pretty much my story and I'm sticking to it.......meaning "I have absolutely nothing else to say about this matter"

Delilah

Dickey's Wedding day

(At the altar...looking at my fiancé...with tears in my eyes)....

I really want to cry right now because...well I'm not attracted to my fiancé...not at all. Damn...I must admit to you that I'm more attracted to her money. If you could only see her...well since you can't, let me describe her to you...she's well...let me be honest with you...she's ugly as hell. She reminds me of a drunk horse...if you've ever seen one that is. I know that sounds cruel...sorry for my honesty. I do love her very much, but I'm not in love with her ...she's just not Delilah.

She has a great heart but it's hard for me to look into her eyes. It's not that I don't want to but damn...her right eye is cockeyed and the left one...it leaks some type of greenish fluid every 15 minutes. The doctor said that eventually it will dry out, but he said that shit 5 years ago. And it's not just her eyes, it's her whole body.

She's 5'4 and 115 pounds… skinny as hell…like a fucking flag pole. She's flat chested…her nipples barely comes off her chest and her ass is flatter than a movie screen. She also has a mole next to her lip (a big fat ass hairy ass mole), she walks with a fucked up limp, and she has the hairiest crotch that I've ever seen. She doesn't like to cut her grass due to her religious beliefs but she allows me to trim it every other month….that way she doesn't feel guilty.

And let's not even talk about the sex!!! Shitttttt!! That's why I have Delilah because my fiancé doesn't like to fuck and when we do…she **ALWAYS** wants me on top. But then she complains that "it hurts when I put it in" so we try doggy style but due to her leg …shit!

Yeah…one of her legs is shorter than the other so she has to wear a special shoe to make her legs have the same length. I need to stop thinking about this because I'm ready to leave her ass right now. But I can't and I won't…she's a good woman and I can't deny that. She treats me well and I shouldn't complain at all.

Even my family asks me why I'm with her. I told them that I love her but they don't believe me. I want to tell them the truth…that I'm with her because she makes great money and our home is beautiful. She's also one hell of a cook…can bake the shit out of a peach cobbler as long as she's focused. You know with both of her eyes I have to watch her ass cook. Sometimes she scares me when she's walking with a knife.

Anyway, we don't have any kids and thankfully she doesn't want any….mainly because her ass can't have any but that's a whole other story right there. I can't even imagine how our kids would look so…

53

(Tasting a little vomit in my mouth)…

But now the wedding has started and I can't help but to think about Delilah. I really want to cry because I can't believe what she's done. It pains me to even think about what Delilah's done to me but I will be okay. I will push forward and marry this woman because the woman that I really wanted to marry Delilah…has hurt me…deeply!

(Breaking down crying)……

Let me get it together but my soon to be wife thinks it's because of her but part of my tears are for her, but the truth is in reality it's because of what Delilah has done to me.

(I feel a snot bubble coming through).

****Reminiscing Alert***Reminiscing Alert***

Well after I left Delilah's house this morning, on our way to the church, I talked to my brother about getting married and explained to him that I wasn't in love with my fiancé. I told him that my heart belongs to Delilah and I couldn't go through with the wedding. Although my brother didn't think that I should dump my fiancé at the altar, I didn't listen to him. All I could do was listen to my heart...and my dick.

"I can't do this! I can't leave Delilah. She's the woman for me, man. Damnit! I really wish that you could understand what I'm going through. Shit. Take me back to her house so I can see her one more time. I need to make sure that she wants me as much as I want her!" And without any hesitation, my brother took me back...to Delilah's apartment.

I was so happy to go back because I had to tell her that I needed her in my life regardless of me being married or not. I just had to because we never discussed what we were going to do after my marriage so I was left confused.

So being the romantic man that I am, I decided not to call her. I mean hell I just left her and figured that she was probably tired from last night with all of the fucking that we had done. I thought that she would be sleep so I decided that I would surprise her and let myself in to her apartment with a key that I secretly copied.

I went to her door and let myself in. When I entered, it was so quiet I decided that I should tiptoe to her bedroom. I wanted to surprise her but instead of me surprising her…I was the one that was surprised.

Her door was closed but not all the way and I heard a man's voice….well I heard his ass moaning and groaning. I recognized that sound. (Sigh) He was getting his dick sucked…by Delilah.

So in my mind I'm thinking…"This bitch just got through fucking me and now she's fucking someone else?"…and as mad as I was becoming, I couldn't say anything. I mean I wanted to say something but I literally couldn't. I was well…I was in fucking shock. But being the dumbass that I am, I didn't leave.

I was shocked but yet curious about who the guy was so for about a good 15 minutes I watched through the crack of the door. All I could see was this guy standing over my girl while she was on her knees sucking his dick. I didn't get to see his face but I did see from the backside was his hairy ass and his nuts dangling from the back! SMH…even I was intimidated by the size of his nuts.

Anyway, he finally came in her mouth (my heart had sank and I wanted to scream) and then she got off her knees and they went to our bed, I mean her bed and started to fuck. He bent Delilah over and he stuck his horse dick inside of her. I'm straight as hell, but his dick was huge. And she took it all in.

He fucked the hell out of her and she enjoyed every moment. She finally came and when he pulled out and headed to the bathroom, that's when I finally got to see the man who she was fucking but what could I say…I tiptoed my ass out of her apartment and trust me I was very hurt. I made it back to the car, with tears in my eyes and I told my brother "Take me to the church. I'm getting married."

Back at the wedding...

And that was it. But the really fucked up part
about all of this is I can't tell my brother
anything because he would just say "I told you
so" and besides that you lose them like you get
them huh? Apparently I had to be reminded that
she was fucking my dad first. But the really
fucked up part about all of this shit right
here...right now is....the man who was fucking
Delilah with the big horse dick and the swollen
balls...well....this motherfucker just told me....

**"We are gathered here today...." The man with
the big balls is Reverend Smalls....**

He can kiss my ass! ☹

Look at his pitiful ass…marrying his sweetheart. Aweee…he's full of shit. He needs to stop that complaining. He's trying to make you (yes you the reader) feel sorry for his ass, but don't. He's not innocent and on top of that bullshit…who told him to go make a fucking key? He shouldn't have done that so that what he gets. And personally I feel violated…him watching me and the pastor…fucking.

Yes Reverend Smalls…….yeah, he does have a big dick. His dick is so big and fat! My pussy is getting wet just thinking about him. But right now I can't think about that. But to give you a little history, Rev. Smalls performed the church service for my dad's funeral and now…he's doing Dickey's wedding.

Anyway, I feel kind of bad. Him having to see me get fucked by another man…ouch! But he will be alright. I wasn't planning on seeing him again after his wedding but I hope that he knows that it's over. And I'm glad that he didn't tell his brother about that incident. I don't want Harry to get upset about me being fucked by the big dick reverend.

(Looking up at Harry…his brother…)

Awe he just blew me a kiss….how sweet.

Dumb fuckers.

Delilah.

Harry
Best man and
Brother....

(At the altar with my brother…staring at the back of his big head…thanking God that this fool is marrying this horse looking woman!)

Now I can be with Delilah and we can finally be seen together. He doesn't know it yet but she's in the church on the back pew. She's fixed up nicely but you can't tell from a distance that it's her. Even Jesus Christ himself wouldn't know who she is…but I know she's here. I just blew her a kiss and she gave me a signal with her hand to let me know that she's here.

I'm crazy about her ass…and her head. Damn she's the best. She should get paid for that shit but let me stop thinking about her and focus on my brother's wedding. Look at him…I can't believe that he's crying but then again I can. His soon-to-be wife's eyes make me want to cry but I just want him to be happy. Although his new wife is ugly as hell, she's a sweet person and I'm glad that she's in the family.

(I've gotten sidetracked…back to the story)…

Fortunately for me, I ended up taking him back to Delilah's house and I thought for a moment that he was going to call the wedding off but with strong conviction he told me to bring him to the church so he can get married. He looked like he had seen a ghost or something, but maybe my baby told him that it was over between them. I didn't ask him any questions…he looked really hurt.

Honestly, I don't even want to know what happened to make him leave like that but I'm sure that she will tell me later. My baby got that magic about her. She's got that special something something that makes me go crazy and I can't wait to put this entire dick inside of her. I love when I beat it from the back…and how she licks my inner thighs while she's sucking my….

Shittttt….let me stop thinking about fucking her. I'm getting on hard just thinking about it, but I'll be with her in about 20 minutes. I can't wait for this day to be over with. I'm ready to show my brother and my family that I've found the love of my life, the woman of my dreams…the squirrel to my nuts! ☺

Poor baby…my poor poor baby. He's up there skinning and grinning not realizing that I've just got through fucking the reverend about a couple of hours ago. Poor thang! If he only knew…hell if all of them knew that the love of their life, the apple of their eyes, and the squirrel to their nuts is really an undercover nympho…they would… I don't want to think of what would do. But it wouldn't be pretty.

Anyway….back to the wedding folks.

Delilah.

Reverend Smalls:
Horse Dick
Thoughts
@ The Altar

(Thinking….)

That damn Delilah! Wow!!! I can't help but to think about her but it's difficult because…right now I'm standing here watching one of the ugliest women I've ever seen and her poor soon to be husband. Look at him…in damn tears! I completely understand why he would be crying. I'm about to cry for him. From the looks of her, their marriage won't last long. I give them about 5 years tops at the most.

I wish that I could stop this charade of a marriage but I can't. It's beyond my duty as a reverend. But what I need to do is to stop thinking about them and think about Delilah. My sweet, precious, delicious Delilah!

****Reminiscing Alert***Reminiscing Alert****

It was like yesterday when I baptized Delilah while her mother and her father watched. She was such a beautiful little girl. Just as sweet as a snicker doodle on a stick. Sometimes I feel bad though…I mean not really but for the record, I'll pretend like I do.

You see her father…well we were best friends back in the day. **(RIP my friend, RIP)** I was friends with her parents ever since high school. I was there since Delilah was born and I got to see Delilah blossom into the beautiful young lady that she is today.

Years had passed and I remember this one particular day when I saw her right after she turned 16. I really looked at her as a grown woman because she looked like she was in her twenties, but I kept that thought to myself. I dared not to mention how beautiful she was to her parents but I told myself, **"When she gets older, I'm going to fuck that tender pussy right there!"** And I never told a soul. I mean really who was I going to tell?

So a few years went by after I had seen her on that faithful day and I wasn't really thinking about how I was going to bed the young lady but low and behold, after she turned 19, she came to visit me by herself… at the church…in my office to talk. She said, "Rev. Smalls…I need to tell you about my dream!"

I then agreed to counsel the young woman…and we had a great conversation. But right now I feel like I'm in a confession because after she told me about her plans for college, she…well…she took her clothes off and jumped on me…naked. I tried to get her off of me. Honestly I did, but if you could've seen the look in her eyes, the size of her nipples and the way that her ass jiggled when she came out of her skirt. I mean she looked great in her white skirt but…
Lord have mercy…

She sat down on my couch and she proceeded to spread her big beautiful thighs and she then did the unthinkable. She started masturbating in my church office. She took her fingers and well...she started to play with her (I need to use a proper word her but pussy keeps coming to my mind) self. Just when she was about to gush all over my couch, she stopped and took my hands and had me to play with her nipples. I couldn't help it...but once I realized that I got caught up...I had to stop.

What would my wife think? What about her father? I mean I stuttered to her "What would Jesus Do??" My goodness...I tried to snatch my hands away from her. I told her "Delilah...no! We can't do this! Your dad would kill..." and I couldn't finish my sentence. She put one of her wet fingers on my lips and said..."Daddy won't know!" and then she preceded to....well...

She kept on insisting that that the Lord told her in a dream that she was to suck my dick...**in order to save the world.** And before you know it, she was on her knees...sucking my dick.

Who was I to be disobedient? The Lord showed her this so...oh my! And me being a man of the cloth, I didn't want the world to end...we had so many lives that we had to save so I had to help her fulfill the prophecy. And we've been saving lives ever since!!!

(Smiling...back to the ceremony)...

I'm just glad that I had enough time to stop by her house and get my blow job that she's been promising me for the last week. My dick is hard as a rock right now just thinking about her and I'm so thankful that I've got on this black robe.

(Silently praising God for it all...including Delilah)...

Anyway, let me get to the ceremony. The music has started and the groom looks like he's ready to kick somebody's ass so...

"We are gathered here today...."

I love Reverend Smalls!! He's my special lover. He gets to lay hands on me all of the time. He's been my rock, my savior, and my lover ever since I was 19 years old. Yeah we've been fucking him for a while now. Shah! He's my little big dick secret and that's how we will keep it okay? But before Dickey came over from his bachelor party, Rev. Smalls popped over to get his dick sucked and he looked so pitiful.

He came over to talk and he told me that he had to perform a wedding tomorrow which is actually today. (I honestly didn't know that he was performing Dickey's wedding...I promise I didn't). He told me that his wife hurt his feelings and he needed to release his anger meaning he needed to fuck.

I told him that he would have to come back over before the ceremony and that I would hook him up. And as usual, like they always do, he showed up today and I hooked him up.
So I couldn't help it...I gave him some pity pussy and a blow job before we both came to this bogus wedding.

But little does Rev. Smalls know that the man he's marrying…is the man that I fucked last night…literally hours before him. Damn…he also doesn't know that the best man who is Dickey's brother…well Reverend Smalls will find out eventually…at the reception. And he doesn't even know that I'm here…

But the Rev. so damn fine….so damn fine!

(Looking at this bitch beside me)….

Damn…this woman next to me is going through it with all of this crying…you would think that we were at a funeral.

(Going through my purse)…

Let me get some tissue for this bitch…she got a little snot running down her nose. I mean she is boo hooing like a motherfucker….

"Here you go Mrs. Smalls. I hope that this helps." (The Rev's wife)…

Lol! I need to head to the restroom…this fiasco of a wedding is over.

Delilah.

Dumb ass Dickey...
Just Married

(Just got done kissing the bride)....

I don't know if she's crying or if her eyes are running, but I'm glad that she's happy because I'm not. I'm still hurt about Delilah and I'm confused as to whether I want to see that bitch again. It took everything in me to not bust Rev. Smalls in the face, but I'm pretty sure he doesn't know that I've been fucking Delilah.

So I can't really be too upset about that. It's just fucking weird how I've just seen this man's dick in her mouth about an hour ago and now he's performing my damn wedding. What kind of sick karma is this? But it's time for us to jump the broom so hold tight until I get back. This shit should be interesting…

(Jumping the broom……..now)……

Okay she tripped up a little bit….you know between her eyes and her legs I knew that this wasn't a bright idea but she wanted it so….but I didn't let her fall and right now we're walking down the aisle while everyone is standing up clapping.

Ughhh…I wish they all would go home but it's time to take pictures and then we are headed to the reception. Although I don't want to be here, I have to pretend that I'm happy for my wife's sake. She deserves better from me and I'm going to do whatever it takes for me to do better by her. But is it still wrong of me to want to see Delilah?

(Walking into the reception hall)…

"It's so beautiful!" my wife said with a kool aid smile. "Yes it is. I love you sweetheart."…I replied as I choked back the tears…..tears of what the fuck am I doing. (sigh) But now the guests are in here as well and everything is going well. My wife and I are about to have our first dance as a married couple. Let me go.

Best man Blues
@ Dickey's Reception

(At the table…watching the bride and groom take their first dance)…

I'm sitting here chilling…waiting on Delilah to text me. I'm looking at my sucker brother dancing with his wife and I still can't believe that he married her. To each his own but if he likes it, then I Lovett. **(Watching my brother dance with his wife)**….I can't wait until Delilah gets here. As much as I love my brother, I can't stand his happy wong tong ass.

He makes me fucking sick….always have, probably always will. He's always been mom's favorite and dad's go to man. I know I shouldn't be mad at my brother, but fuck it…it is what it is. Anyway, let me go to the bathroom and text Delilah. I know her ass is here. She's getting worse with this texting shit.

(Walking out now)….

(In the bathroom)…

I can't believe that I'm hearing some damn moaning and groaning in the church bathroom. Damn……sounds like somebody is fucking or getting their dick sucked. What the hell! **(Laughing in my head)…**Of all the places in the world, I can't believe that someone would find it appropriate to have sex in a church bathroom. Hmmm…I tell ya.

This world is going to hell in a hand basket. But I won't interrupt them. I'm kind of jealous and it sounds like he's getting it in. Would I be wrong if I take a peek?   Damn…I have to at least see the man shoes or something…I'm nosey and jealous…hold on (looking through the crack of the bathroom door)…oh yeah…he's getting it in but I can't see her at all. I hope it's a woman sucking his dick.

I wish I could tell that brother to bust one for me but I guess I'll have to wait on Delilah tonight. I'm going to step out and let them have their privacy. It's making me think about when Delilah was giving me head in a club bathroom the other night. It was so fucking good! Oh yeah before I forget…let me text this woman.

Hold tight one minute**…. texting her now…."Where are you? I'm waiting on you. Please call me when you get this message. Can't wait to see you!!** (Adjusting my dick…it's starting to get on hard) I can't wait to see her but let me get out of here….my dick is getting hard just listening to these two fucking in the stall.

Shit...my phone just went off. I can't answer it right now because I'm busy... sucking Reverend Smalls dick...in the bathroom...in the church. Damn. Hold on while I finish him off. I tried to resist sucking his dick in church but I couldn't help it. The reverend has a really big dick and well...you know how I do it. Anyway, he's about to cum and I want to catch it in my mouth so hold on...

(Damn...he's holding my head so fucking tight while he's nutting in my mouth...he's about to squeeze my fucking brains out of my head)....

(10 minutes later)....

Okay Rev. Smalls has came, saw and fucking conquered. He sneaked me out of the bathroom and now we're headed into the reception so I'm done. I couldn't text Harry back, but I'm sending him a text now. When I see him I'll let him know that I was talking to Rev. Smalls about getting baptized. Don't fucking laugh....I'm the perfect candidate for being saved. LOL!

Delilah.

Back to the best man...

81

(Sitting in the hallway…)

I'm still waiting on her ass but she just sent me a text letting me know that she's on her way. Instead of waiting on her in the reception hall, I decided that I would meet her in the hallway so we can walk into the reception together. That way I can hold her hand and walk in with her to make it fucking clear to everyone in the room that this is my woman.

It's been about fifteen minutes and now she's walking up to me. **(Hugging her)…**I'm kissing her on her perfect brown lips and boy I want to take her in the bathroom and get my dick sucked….like the lucky guy who was in there earlier.

For a moment I forgot that I was in a church and I'm going to respect that although some dumb ass couple was getting it in. It seems to me that they would have enough respect for the man upstairs but hey who am I to judge. I'm just gonna wait to get home to fuck the shit out of Delilah.

"Hey babe. Where have you been? I've been waiting so long for you to get here."…I asked her. I put her in my arms again because I'm kind of scared to let her go. I'm very insecure when it comes to Delilah and I want to do whatever it takes to keep her.

Right now she's explaining to me that she's been with Reverend Smalls talking about getting baptized. She's saying that before we can move further in our relationship, she wants to move closer to Jesus. And I totally respect that. "Speaking of Rev. Smalls, here he is. Would you like to meet him?"…she said.

"Of course babe! I would love to meet the man who just married my brother…and who's going to baptize you."…I replied. She is blowing my mind…like she blows my dick. I'm just so impressed with the fact that she's ready to get her life together and have a relationship with the man upstairs.

(Reverend Smalls walking up to us...with his right hand out and the bible in his left hand)....

"Hi...I'm Harry. How are you? You must be Reverend Smalls"....as I'm shaking hands and I've just introduced myself. He's a good looking older guy...he wouldn't be Delilah's type at all though. She doesn't go for the old men. "Delilah is a wonderful young lady and I look forward to re-baptizing her very soon. You are a lucky man to have her."...he said and then he flashed me his pearly smile.

Feeling kind of awkward because I never knew that Delilah was ever baptized in the first place and it's something about his smile that didn't quite seem right. He's making me feel uncomfortable right now. He seems like an hmmm...I can't quite put my finger on him but I'm sizing his ass up right now.

(Looking at his haircut, clothing, his jewelry...)

Okay the Rev doesn't do bad in the money arena. He's got on nice clothes and jewelry but something just told me to look at his shoes and damn...I recognize his shoes. Ain't that some shit! I'm smiling cause I can't believe that it was the Rev getting his dick sucked. It was the Reverend in his church bathroom getting it in.

(Smile fading away...)

But I'm about two seconds from knocking this motherfucker's teeth in because what I really can't believe is...I just saw Delilah's shoes next to his...which are the same damn shoes I saw in the bathroom stall ...who was sucking the reverend's dick. Yeah I looked under the stall to see their shoes!!!! What the fuck?

I guess this motherfucker can count. He put two and two together…which gave him 4 shoes. I'm trying to figure out how in the hell did he see my shoes? I'm kind of speechless and I don't know what I'm going to say to him. I don't know what to say to him or how to explain why the Reverend's dick was in my mouth.

Thankfully the wedding is over and we never made it to the reception. I told him that I had an emergency and that I needed to leave. He said he understood but he looked kind of pissed off so…he called me about an hour ago and said that he wanted to talk to me…in person. So now I'm at home waiting for him to come over and I don't know what to say to him. I'm really worried…

(Ding dong, ding dong)….

He's here. Hold tight I'll be right back.

(Answering the door...they left)...

I'm back but I need to make a quick phone call. There was an idiot at my door. Hold on for a few minutes...

(Picking up the phone...dialing)...

911: Nine One One Operator 6100~What's your emergency?

Me: Operator....

911: Are you there? What's your emergency?

Me: I've been sttttaaabbed....

911: Where's your location maam?

Me: I'm at....68 Glen Knoll Rd...can you hurry up? I'm bleeding....

911: Do you know who stabbed you?

Me: Yes... I do... (pause)

911: Maam....you there?

Me: (long pause)...Yes...It was my mother...fuckkkkkkkinggggg....
(Phone drops)....

Until the next time....

Delilah

One last thought: Just in case this bitch goes to meet Jesus!

The first time I saw her…well she did something to me. I honestly can say that I loved her too… the first moment that I laid eyes on her at her father's funeral. I didn't know who she was at the time but her beauty captivated me.

I knew all the men wanted to know who she was when she walked in. That's how beautiful she was…she managed to make most of us forget that we were in a church…at a funeral. But there she was…in all white….with her grandmother. They sat there and well I just knew that I needed to be with her.

So after the funeral, I met her and well…we exchanged numbers. I had to call her that day…the same day of the funeral but I had to have her. I had to be a part of her world. And well…the next week we met…and made love all day long. And now….we are still lovers. I only wish that I could tell my husband that…I'm sleeping with his **half-sister**.

(10 minutes later...still waiting on the fucking cops)....

In a world full of heroes, I need one right now. I don't need another fucking person to express their love for me. I just hope that this bitch doesn't say anything to him. That shit will destroy him. And that's another book called "Her Thoughts, Her Thighs" v.1...for the lady lickers in the world. But right now...

(Police walking through the door)...

These motherfuckers are finally here. Pray for me!

Delilah.

"If you really want to know if this trifling bitch is dead or not, pick up volume 3....coming soon!!!"

~~

www.BetrayalBooks.com

Also, forgive us for the errors but we hope that you enjoyed the book.

Made in the USA
Columbia, SC
31 October 2024

45419100R00059